Tall Tales of Old India from a Very, Very, Very Long Time Ago

MONKEY AND CROCODILE
The Panchatantra Book Four Retold

Narindar Uberoi Kelly

Illustrated by Meagan Jenigen

For my grandson Jandiga Kelly Holmes

Order this book online at www.trafford.com
or email orders@trafford.com

Most Trafford titles are also available at major online book retailers.

Printed in the United States of America.

ISBN: 978-1-4907-4039-3 (sc)
978-1-4907-4042-3 (e)

Trafford rev. 07/10/2014

 www.trafford.com

North America & international
toll-free: 1 888 232 4444 (USA & Canada)
fax: 812 355 4082

Note To The Reader

I fell in love with these stories as a tween who stumbled across them in a library at a time when my family were refugees as a result of the partition of India between what is now Pakistan and India. I suppose part of the attraction of the stories was escape from the realities of being homeless in a part of India that seemed a different country, with people speaking different languages and eating food quite unlike anything I was used to. But the stories helped me by giving me some insight into what and why my parents were trying to teach me—and some appreciation for what I was resisting in a world turned upside down by our narrow escape from the violence and turmoil of our loss of home and country.

I decided I wanted my grandchildren to have access to these stories that meant so much to me, but in a language that they could easily understand. As I adapted the stories for modern readers, it occurred to me one of the great strengths of the Panchatantra (literally the five books) derives from what at first seems the sheer nonsense of listening in to animals talking like humans. Yet this absurd conceit of animals chatting and arguing and telling stories immediately establishes a strangely safe distance between the reader and these creatures. And even more strangely, we are transformed into observers and compatriots in their struggles with thorny issues of friendship, collaboration, conflict and ambition. If I was particularly taken with these tales at a time of vulnerability and uncertainty in my life, readers approaching and experiencing adolescence and young maturity (when *does* that process end?) are in some sense similarly adrift and puzzled by the strange new land of adulthood. Readers of these tales are assumed to be much like I was--expatriates operating in a new landscape they don't fully understand.

The genius of these stories is their relentless unwillingness to whitewash or romanticize adult life. They depict the ignoble as well as the noble, cruelty and deceit as well as honor, foolishness as much as cunning, deception as rampant as honesty. They show the underside as well as glimpses of fulfillment in adult life. The stories unveil the contradictory nature of adult life, its tensions, risks and dangers as well as its rewards. And it accomplishes this through the disorienting welter of stories within stories that pile up on each other to convey a kind of confusion that forms a powerful antidote to other literary forms designed to convey wisdom—like preaching, teaching, telling people what to do. Out of this confusion, somehow wisdom can escape as a form of deeper appreciation of the perils and tensions and value of leading a good life.

Narindar Uberoi Kelly

TALL TALES OF OLD INDIA

There was a king called Immortal-Power who lived in a fabulous city which had everything. He had three sons. They were truly ignorant. The King saw that they could not figure things out and did not want to learn. They hated school. So the King asked a very wise man to wake up their brains. The wise man, a Brahmin named Sharma, took the three Princes to his home. Every day he told them stories that taught the Princes lessons on how to live intelligently. To make sure they would never forget he made them learn the stories by heart. The fourth set of teaching tales Sharma told were:

Monkey and Crocodile

Sharma began

"Only a fool parts with gains
When sweet-talked out of them
And then must pay the price
The Monkey exacted from
The Crocodile."

"How come?" asked the three Princes, and Sharma told this story.

MONKEY AND CROCODILE

The Panchatantra Book Four Retold

Narindar Uberoi Kelly

Illustrated by Meagan Jenigen

Monkey and Crocodile

Introduction

Story	Told By	To
Monkey and Crocodile	Sharma, Teacher	The Three Princes
Vindictive Frog-King	Ruddy, Monkey	Oily, Crocodile
Donkey Long Ears and Jackal Muddy	Ruddy, Monkey	Oily, Crocodile
Feisty Potter	Ruddy, Monkey	Oily, Crocodile
Jackal Raised By a Lioness	Honest, Potter	The King
Ungrateful Wife	Ruddy, Monkey	Oily, Crocodile
Two Hen-Pecked Husbands	Ruddy, Monkey	Oily, Crocodile
Ass in the Tiger-Skin	Ruddy, Monkey	Oily, Crocodile
Aged Farmer's Young Wife	Oily, Crocodile	Ruddy, Monkey
Meddling Sparrow-Hen	Ruddy, Monkey	Oily, Crocodile
How the Wily Jackal Ate the Elephant	Ruddy, Monkey	Oily, Crocodile
Dog Who Went Abroad	Ruddy, Monkey	Oily, Crocodile

INTRODUCTION

The purpose of these stories has always been to teach basic knowledge and wisdom that makes for a better life. Each of the five 'books' in the original were organized around a theme: Loss of Friends, Making of Friends, War or Peace, Loss of Gains, Ill-considered Action.

Book Four here titled simply 'Monkey and Crocodile' deals with how to protect and preserve any gains you have made in life, no matter in what sphere. Most of the loss-of-gain stories are told by the Monkey who fooled the Crocodile into freeing him from sure death by telling a clever story. Many of the Monkey's stories are about the use of deceit to improve one's position, or to protect oneself. And the losers are foolish enough to be tricked out of their gains by a sweet-talking adversary. They are gullible and deserve what they get. Husbands will, apparently, do anything for their wives and sometimes pay a heavy price. And wives – like the Crocodile's wife in the frame story – are typically characterized as demanding and unreasonable. Deceit, when exposed, can lead to the deceiver's undoing. One should be humble before the noble, use intrigue when one cannot win advantage by strength, pay bribes when necessary, pick a fight only with equals, and give good advice only to those best able to use it.

The *frame* story then is about the Monkey and the Crocodile. They discuss the situation they are in and justify their viewpoints through tales that form most of the book's *nesting* stories. These, mostly single stand-alone stories, are separated in this presentation from the main one by a simple conceit: the frame story of the two friends become adversaries is located on the left hand pages with the text enclosed within a 'frame' and can be read without interruption, while the pages on the right side of the open book tell the stand-alone and nesting stories. This allows parents reading aloud to young children, or young adults, or adults of any age, to choose how they want to read the book – just the frame story or just selected nesting stories, or both left and right of the open pages to experience the original design of the book.

A word of caution: some of these stories illustrate Indian practices of many centuries past. Women are not often depicted or treated well, a phenomenon that continues to this day. But the stories have much to tell us. I trust that parents will help their children to understand the age-old realities described in this book and use the occasion to teach their own values.

Monkey and Crocodile

There was a great big rose-apple tree that grew close to the bank of an enormous river. It always had delicious fruit which ripened every day and was much enjoyed by a red-faced monkey who was named Ruddy. One day a crocodile named Oily, crawled out of the river onto the bank and burrowed into the soft sand. Ruddy saw him and welcomed his guest "No one is more important than a guest to me no matter how unexpected. Please accept these scrumptious rose-apples that I throw down to you as my offering." The crocodile Oily enjoyed them very much, spent time in easy conversation with Ruddy, and took some rose-apples home to his wife. "Where did you find these?" she asked Oily. "They are like ambrosia". "I have made a new friend, Ruddy, and he gets them from the tree and gives them to me" replied Oily. Then the wife reasoned that if the monkey ate such heavenly fruit every day, he must have a heart with unearthly powers. So she said to Oily "If you value me at all, please bring me the monkey's heart so that when I eat it I will never grow old or sick but will be your loving wife forever." Oily objected strongly. "Ruddy is like a brother to me now and remember brothers by friendship are even more precious than brothers by birth. He gives me fruit every day. I cannot kill him!" But the wife was adamant "You have never said No to me before. You must love this she-monkey more than me and if this is a male-monkey, why do you love him? Monkeys and crocodiles are natural enemies. Bring me his heart or I will die of starvation for I will eat nothing else." Completely dejected, Oily returned to the rose-apple tree thinking "how can I possibly kill my friend?"

Ruddy had missed his friend Oily the crocodile so upon seeing him return said cheerfully "What shall we discuss today as we eat the rose-apples?" "My wife is very upset that I have not invited you home" replied Oily. "She has prepared a great welcome for you. So come with me." Ruddy was delighted and replied "I hold the six aspects of friendship very dear: to receive, to give, to listen, to talk, to dine, and to entertain. But we monkeys live in trees and you live in water. How can I come to your house? Please bring your wife here." "Our house is on a sandbank" said Oily "and you will be quite comfortable there. No need to worry. Just climb on my back and I will take you there." So Ruddy climbed upon the crocodile's back, but when Oily took off at considerable speed, Ruddy was frightened and asked Oily to slow down. But Oily knew that Ruddy was out of his depth in the fast moving water and now completely in his power. He could not stop himself from bragging "My wife wants to eat your heart. Better say your last prayers!" Ruddy was however very quick-witted and said immediately "Why didn't you tell me on the shore? I have a second heart that I keep in my hole in the rose-apple tree. That is my sweet heart. The heart I carry around is very ordinary and will not do your wife any good." Oily was delighted. Now he could give his wife the monkey's sweet heart and still have a friend. So he turned back to shore and helped Ruddy climb high up the rose-apple tree. Ruddy, meanwhile was thinking *one should never be too trusting*. I have evaded death and thus am reborn today.

After waiting a while Oily shouted up to Ruddy "Give me the heart so I can appease my wife and be back for our regular time conversing about interesting things." "You are not only a traitor but a fool!" said Ruddy. "How can anyone have two hearts? Don't ever come back here. Remember the proverb *If you trust a faithless friend twice, death is as certain as a mule conceiving*." Oily tried once more to win Ruddy back: "I was just trying to test you. It was all a joke. Just come with me and be a guest in our home." "Go away!" said Ruddy "Remember the story of Mr. Handsome and the Frog-King." "Tell me, tell me" said the Crocodile and the Monkey told this story.

Vindictive Frog-King

There was a Frog-King who lived in a well with a water-wheel. He was sick of having relatives beg him for favors and decided to leave the well. He hopped carefully from bucket to bucket of the water wheel and succeeded in getting out of the deep well. Once out, however, the Frog-King began to brood on how to get even with his relatives. Payback makes men feel good. Just then he noticed a sleek but deadly black snake that people had nick-named Mr. Handsome. I know, he said to himself, I will lead this snake into my well and he will exterminate all my awful relatives who made my life so miserable. They do say the wise use one foe to destroy another. So the Frog-King approached Mr. Handsome and made his proposition to him. Mr. Handsome was doubtful. He and the Frog-King were natural enemies but the Frog-King convinced him that the deal could only benefit Mr. Handsome because the Frog-King promised to give the serpent one frog a day. Mr. Handsome agreed and made his way down to the bottom of the well with the help of the Frog-King. But, of course he did not stop with the destruction of the frogs that the Frog-King wanted killed as payback. One day Mr. Handsome ate the Frog-King's own son. The Queen was horrified and blamed the Frog-King. "No point in howling now! Find a way for us to escape or think of a way to kill the serpent." Eventually only the Frog-King was left alive, so Mr. Handsome said to him "Friend, all the frogs are gone and I am hungry. Get me some food." "No problem" said the Frog-King. "If you allow me, I shall go to another well and lure all the frogs living there to come over to this well." Mr. handsome was delighted. "You have been a brother to me. So go off and may you succeed in your scheme." The Frog-King finally escaped from the well and went as far away as he could.

After a very long time, Mr. Handsome saw a lizard in the well and asked her for a favor. "Pretty please, go look for the Frog-King and tell him I miss him and even if he comes alone I promise not to hurt him on pain of burning in hell in my after life." The lizard delivered the message to the Frog-King who said "Go, fair lady, and tell Mr. Handsome, the Frog-King will never return to the well."

"And that is why" said Ruddy "I will never enter your home."
"Please, please, " said Oily "If you don't come I will sit here and
starve to death." "You idiot!" said Ruddy "Am I like Long Ears that
I will go to a place of obvious certain death?" "What happened to
Long Ears?" asked Oily and Ruddy told this story.

Long Ears and Muddy

A lion named Ferocious lived in a jungle with his loyal servant, a jackal named Muddy. One day Ferocious had a nasty fight with an elephant and was badly wounded. Since the lion could not go hunting and kill animals for food, poor Muddy also had to do without. When he could take it no more, he said to his master "O King, I can barely move from hunger, so how should I serve you?" Ferocious replied "Bring me an animal that I can kill, even in my present condition."

So Muddy went hunting near a village and came across a donkey named Long Ears who was himself weak and thin and having trouble munching on tough grasses. Muddy approached Long ears and asked "How did you get so weak?" "I have a terrible master" replied Long Ears. "He overloads me and doesn't feed me enough. So I eat these tough grasses but they do not agree with me". Muddy offered "Come live with me. I know a spot with soft green grass by the river." "But I cannot live in a forest; the forest animals will kill me" said Long ears. But Muddy was a clever jackal and succeeded in luring the poor Donkey to the forest by promising him a beautiful female donkey for a wife. Long Ears went into the Lion's den but Ferocious, in his eagerness to kill, somehow overshot his spring and the Donkey escaped. Then Muddy asked Ferocious "What on earth happened?" "I had no time to prepare my spring. You had better get me another animal." "You prepare a better spring for I will get Long Ears to come back" said Muddy. "How can you entice Long Ears back when he saw the danger first hand?" asked Ferocious. "Never you mind" said the Jackal and went after the Donkey. "Long Ears, you must return. The fearsome animal you saw was just a she-donkey in heat. You are shy but you should not have run away." So the gullible Long Ears returned with Muddy to the Lion's den a second time and was killed instantly by Ferocious. But before feasting on him Ferocious decided to go bathe in the river and left Muddy in charge of the kill. When he returned, it was clear that the jackal had already feasted on the heart and ears of the donkey. Ferocious shouted angrily "You rogue, you have eaten the best parts and left your leavings for your Master!" Muddy was ready with his response "O King, the Donkey had no heart or ears, otherwise he would not have forgotten his fear and returned to face certain death." Ferocious accepted the explanation and they dined together.

"I am NOT Long Ears" continued Ruddy to Oily. "You played a
trick on me but then spoiled it by telling the truth so you lost
your gains just like Feisty, the Potter." "How was that?" asked
the Crocodile, and the Monkey told this story.

Feisty Potter

Once there was a potter named Honest, who had a terrible accident. He cut his forehead open very badly falling over one of his broken pots with a jagged edge. The cut healed but Honest looked horribly ugly.

One year when his business as a potter was failing and there was a famine, Honest decided to leave his area and become a life guard elsewhere. In his new hometown the King saw him, noticed his scar, and concluded Honest must be a war hero. Believing this, he showed the Potter great respect, showered him with honors and gifts until even his own sons became jealous although they kept quiet.

A day came when the King was reviewing his premier troop battalion. Around him elephants and horses were being readied for battle. The King saw the potter among the spectators and asked him "Prince, who are you? What is your family? In what war were you wounded?" Honest readily explained how he got his horrible scar. The King was so angry at his own mistake that he immediately ordered a flogging for Honest. After which the Potter said to the King "Please your Majesty, don't treat me like this but check out how good I am in battle." The King answered "Be gone. You may be handsome, brave and bright, but in your family no elephants are slain." "How so?" asked Honest and the King told this story.

Jackal Raised By A Lioness

A Lion lived in a dense forest with his mate. Time passed and the Lioness gave birth to twin cubs. The parents were pleased and raised them together, the Lion providing the food and the Lioness the caring for the cubs. One day the Lion searched far and wide but could find no food for his family. On the way back to his den he came upon a scrawny baby jackal. Full of pity, the Lion picked him up from the scruff of his neck and took him home for his wife to take care of raising him. They both knew they could not eat him. They knew that the gods frowned on anyone who strikes a holy man, a woman or a child and the baby jackal was like a child. So the baby Jackal grew up in the Lion family thinking the Lion cubs were his brothers and he began behaving like them.

When the cubs were half grown, a wild elephant came wandering. The two Lion cubs were eager to try their strength and wanted to kill the elephant. But the Jackal said "The elephant is an enemy of our race. Leave him alone" and ran home as fast as he could.

Later the Lion Cubs told their mother what happened. The Jackal felt humiliated. He was so angry that he wanted to kill his own brothers and said so to his mother. While she tried to calm him down, the Lioness realized it was time to give her adopted cub the unvarnished truth. "You are handsome, brave and bright, but in your birth family, my boy, no elephants were ever slain. You are a jackal raised by a lioness. It is time now to return to your own kind." The poor Jackal left immediately. "That is why, you poor potter" said the King "I suggest you leave right away before the other soldiers make fun and kill you." The Potter fled.

"You really are a fool" Ruddy continued chiding Oily "*Never trust a woman*. Remember the plight of the man who left his family and gave half his life to his wife who left him without a single thought." "How so?" asked the Crocodile, and the Monkey told this story.

Ungrateful Wife

A long time ago there lived a Brahmin who loved his wife more than life itself. But she had a nasty temper and quarreled every day with one or other of the extended family members with whom the couple lived after they were married. The poor Brahmin found the situation intolerable and eventually left his family to go live elsewhere, far away.

On the way they had to pass through a great forest. The Wife said to her husband that she was very thirsty and could he please get her some water. When the Brahmin returned with some water, he found his Wife lying on the ground, dead. Stricken with overwhelming grief, he immediately started praying. He begged the Gods to give him back his Wife no matter what the cost. "Even half your life?" was the answer from on high and he said "Yes" quite happily. He was instructed to recite required prayers and say "I give life" three times. Lo and behold his Wife got better and they continued their journey.

When they reached the outskirts of a town, the Brahmin asked his wife to wait at the gates where there was a nice park while he went in search for food. When he was gone, the Wife met a handsome young cripple and fell in love at first sight. She seduced him to make love to her and when the husband returned she asked him to help carry the cripple so they could be a three-some. Thoroughly confused, the Brahmin objected saying "I can barely carry myself, how can I carry him?" The Wife, however, offered to carry the cripple in a basket on her head to which the bewildered husband agreed and they continued their journey to town.

When the Wife noticed a well near the path they were travelling, she signaled her lover to help push the Brahmin into the well which they did! Having got rid of the husband, the Wife walked on towards the center of the town with her lover still in the basket which she carried on her head. But she came up to a toll gate where the guards asked her to pay toll for whatever she had in the basket. When she wouldn't, they took the covered basket to the King and the Wife followed. When she was in the presence of the King, she concocted a story. "Your Majesty, the cripple is my husband. First my relatives married me to him but then so mistreated him and me that I had to leave. My love and honor for my husband would not allow me to leave him behind. So I carry him in a basket on my head." The King was so touched by the love story that he gave her and the cripple a couple of villages so they could live comfortably.

But the Brahmin was not dead. He managed to get out of the well and went after his Wife and lover. Their quarrel brought them before the King once again. The Wife, of course, accused the husband of being one of the relatives who mistreated her and the cripple. The Brahmin, however kept his cool when the King was about to order his execution. He said "Your Majesty, my wife, this woman, has something that belongs to me. For the sake of justice, would you please order her to return it so I can die happy?" The King granted his last request and the Brahmin asked his Wife to return the half of his life he had given her. Although she protested loudly that she had nothing of his, the Brahmin said his prayers and asked his Wife to repeat "I give life" three times. Since the Wife dare not refuse the King's order she did what the Brahmin asked and after she had spoken she fell down dead. The King was astonished and wanted to hear a full explanation that the Brahmin happily gave. She was an ungrateful wife

Having told the story, Ruddy went on "But there is another tale even more apt for highlighting the same moral. Men will do anything if asked by a wife: like shaving their heads out of season, or saying anything even neighing like a horse." "What are you talking about? Tell me" said the Crocodile and the Monkey told this story.

Two Hen-Pecked Husbands

Once there was a King named Magnificent renowned for his wealth and power. He had a minister named Meritorious, whom he trusted and who was extremely learned in all the arts and sciences. But each had a problem.

The Minister adored his wife but even he had a lover's quarrel one day, and his wife would no longer speak to him. He begged her forgiveness and promised he would do whatever she asked. His Wife eventually relented but conditionally, and he had to shave his head for her to start talking to him again.

The King also got into an argument with the Queen. Although it was a trivial matter she stopped speaking to him. He asked her pardon for his part in the argument and asked what he could do as penance. The Queen thought it over and said "If you pretend to be a horse, take a horse's bit in your mouth, let me ride you and neigh when I take the whip to you, all shall be forgiven."

*

Having told the story, Ruddy continued to rebuke Oily. "You are an idiot! You too are hen-pecked like the King and his Minister. You undertook to kill me because your wife demanded it. You said so yourself. Remember parrots and myna birds are caged because they mimic words. Even the well-disguised ass was killed because he opened his mouth." "How was that?" asked the Crocodile, and the Monkey told this story.

Ass In The Tiger Skin

There was a laundry man named Clean White, who lived in a small town. He had a donkey who had grown thin and weak because the owner Clean White was unable to give him good feed. One day Clean White was wandering in a nearby forest when he saw a dead tiger. He immediately wondered how could he use the tiger skin? He devised a plan to dress his donkey in the tiger skin and let him go out at night to graze in the neighnors barley fields. He was sure that when the watchful farmers saw a tiger in their fields they would leave him alone. So Clean White took the dead tiger home and skinned it.

The laundry man's plan worked perfectly: the donkey could feed well every night, became quite fat, and could do good work for Clean White during the day. Time passed and one night when the ass in the tiger skin was eating in the barley fields he heard the call of a she-donkey in the distance. So, of course, the donkey brayed in answer. The farmers realized that the tiger they were avoiding was just a disguised donkey. They were very angry, caught the donkey and killed it.

*

Now, while the Monkey Ruddy was telling the Crocodile Oily the story, a small water-dweller came up the river bank with a message for the Crocodile. "Your wife has starved herself to death." Poor Oily became confused and dejected: "Oh dear, oh dear, what will become of me? The proverb says a home without a mother or a wife is no use and it is safer to leave it. Ruddy, my friend, forgive my sins against you. Now that she is gone I will burn myself alive." Ruddy laughed and said "Come, come. You are just proving that you are a hen-pecked fool. One should celebrate when a wife like yours dies. As the wise men say, an ever-carping, ever-nagging wife should be shunned at all costs." "But what am I to do?" cried the Crocodile. "I have lost my wife and my friend, two disasters at once. But I suppose I should remember the wife who lost her husband and her lover and had only a vacant stare." "How was that?" asked the Monkey, and the Crocodile told this story.

22

Aged Farmer's Young Wife

There was an old but well to do farmer who had a small farm where he lived with his much younger wife. The Wife was bored and discontented and always on the lookout for a lover. One day when she was in a nearby village, a small time but very handsome con man noticed her and thought he would try his luck with her. He approached her and said "This is love at first sight. Will you be mine?" The Wife saw how young and beautiful he was. She couldn't resist him and recklessly decided to run off with him. "My husband is very old and pretty wealthy. Wait here for me and I will go collect some valuables and we will go to some other village and live happily."

The young rogue waited and the Wife returned with a large portion of her husband's money and valuables. Together they started on their journey. Eventually they had to cross a river. Immediately the young man, who was after all a habitual criminal, made a plan to rob the woman and run. "The water in the river is deep and the current here is quite strong. Perhaps I should go first with our belongings, leave them on the opposite bank and return to carry you across." When she gave him all the valuables, he suggested she also give him her outer garments so she would be lighter when he carried her across. The besotted woman did what he asked her to do. So the rogue gathered his loot, swam across the river never to return.

Eventually, the farmer's Wife realized what had happened. Dejected she sat and stared at the river. Presently a female jackal came by with a chunk of raw meat in her mouth and saw a big fish leap out of the river and land on the bank. The jackal dropped the meat and sprang for the fish but missed. The fish wiggled back into the water and swam away. While the jackal was watching the fish a vulture swooped down from the sky above, snatched the meat, and flew away. The practically naked woman smiled and mocked the jackal "So what do you wish for now that you have lost meat and fish?" The she-jackal replied "You are at least twice as clever as me, yet all you have is a vacant stare having lost both husband and lover."

*

While Oily was telling the story, yet another water-dweller brought a message for Oily: "Your home has been taken over by a very big crocodile." Hearing this, the Crocodile said "A strong stranger has taken my house, my friend is mad at me and my wife is dead. Bad things don't happen one at a time. What shall I do? Try to recover my house by confrontation, conciliation, intrigue or bribery. Please, Ruddy, advise me." But the Monkey retorted "You ungrateful fool! I have told you to go away. Why pursue me? Why should I give you good advice? *One should only give good advice to people best able to use it.* Remember the foolish monkey who destroyed the sparrow's cozy nest." "How was that?" asked the Crocodile, and the Monkey told this Story.

Meddling Sparrow-Hen

A Sparrow and his wife had built their cozy little nest on a branch of a tree. Underneath it, in the middle of winter, a Monkey took shelter. He had been caught in a hail-storm and was wet and shivering. His teeth chattered and his hands and feet were numb. The Sparrow-Hen saw his miserable plight and said "You have hands and feet like a man, so why don't you build a house for yourself, you fool!" The Monkey was irritated and thought to himself, everyone thinks they know best. To the Sparrow-Hen he said "Miss Smarty Pants! Hush up or I will spoil your party." But the interfering Sparrow-hen continued to give him excellent advice on how to build a house even when the Monkey had clearly told her to leave him alone. Eventually he got so mad that he shook the branch she lived on and destroyed her nest.

Having heard the story, the Crocodile still persisted. "Oh my friend, I know I did you wrong. But we were good friends once so, for old time's sake, please advise me." "I will not tell you to do one thing" said Ruddy. "You took your wife's advice and took me on your back under false pretenses to drop me in the river. Even if you loved your wife, why hurt your friends and relatives because she asked you?" Oily still continued "I beg you to forgive. You know men who give wise advice don't ever suffer here or hereafter." "Oh, all right," said Ruddy at last. "You had better go and fight the usurper for *it is said that one should be humble before the noble, use intrigue against heroes, give petty bribes to lackeys, but fight it out with equals.*" "Tell me the tale" begged the Crocodile, and the Monkey told this story.

How the Wily Jackal Ate the Elephant

A very clever jackal named Wily lived by his wits in a dense forest. One day he found an elephant that had died that day from natural causes. The Jackal tried to bite through the thick hide to get at the meat but could not do so.

Presently, a Lion wandered into the copse where the elephant lay. Quickly, Wily bowed low to the ground and said "O King, I have been standing guard over your elephant. Please eat as much as is to your liking." "I never eat what I have not killed myself" replied the Lion. "I give the elephant to you", and he left.

As soon as the Lion had gone, a Tiger appeared. Smart Wily figured he needed a different strategy. Being humble had worked with the Lion, intrigue would probably work better this time. "O Sir, please beware. This elephant was killed just now by a Lion. He left me to keep guard and has gone to bathe in the river before having his meal. He did say before he left that if a Tiger came by, I was to go at once to warn him for he intends to kill all tigers in this forest as revenge for the one tiger who stole his previous kill, giving him only the leavings." The Tiger fled for his life.

No sooner had the Tiger left than the Leopard arrived. Wily accosted him as a friend. "I haven't seen you in ages. You are a welcome guest. Please help yourself to the elephant just killed by the Lion. I am appointed to guard it but the Lion won't be back for a while. As my guest, help yourself and if I signal the Lion is near, then run." The Leopard was hesitant but Wily persuaded him to have a bite. Once the Leopard had made a deep cut in the elephant hide with his powerful fangs, the jackal gave the signal and the Leopard ran away.

When, finally, Wily was about to feast on the elephant, another jackal arrived. Wily recalled the maxim: bow to your superior, be devious facing the valiant, give bribes to the lower classes, confront your equals. Wily rushed menacingly at the other jackal and easily killed him. Then he sat down and ate the elephant in comfort.

*

"So, my advice is go fight with the other crocodile. You are equals. If you don't, he will destroy you eventually. Remember, even if you leave and go abroad, your kind there will still be a problem." "How so?" asked the Crocodile, and the Monkey told this story.

The Dog Who Went Abroad

A dog named Curly lived comfortably in a small town until a prolonged famine occurred. All the dogs and other domestic animals felt the scarcity of food. Many became thin and weak like Curly. Many starved to death. Curly decided to leave and go abroad to a city he had heard about.

Once he arrived in the foreign city, he met a generous lady who invited him to her house. He began going there regularly, was very well fed and put on weight. But every time he left her door, he was surrounded by local dogs, powerful and proud, who often encircled him with obvious menace and occasionally attacked him. Eventually he got fed up with his situation and returned home.

His kinsman and friends who had survived the famine came running to greet him and ask him lots of questions. They were full of curiosity about his experiences abroad. So Curly recounted "There was plenty of good food, many easygoing women. Only one thing was wrong. My own kind hated my guts for joining them there."

After listening to his friend's advice, Oily the Crocodile decided to go home to oust the stranger who had taken over his house. He confronted and fought the interloper with courage and valor and was victorious. He killed the usurper of his home and lived there in comfort for many years.

ACKNOWLEDGEMENTS

As I have noted elsewhere, the *Panchatantra* stories (literally Five Books) have been part of India's oral and scholarly tradition for at least two thousand years or more. They have been told and retold all over the world and have influenced many literary genres, particularly those containing animal characters and 'nesting stories' i.e. one story in another story in another story. Sometime towards the end of the twelfth century, the seminal version of the *Panchatantra* was written by Vishnusharma in Sanskrit and has formed the best known rendition ever since. It is comprised of a vast array of folk wisdom interspersed with eighty-five stories which collectively serve as a guide book of sorts on how to live a wise and good life. Many translations of the text are available in English and some selected stories have been published for young children. However, the entire collection has never been adapted for casual readers, whether teenagers or adults.

My goal is to make the core of the *Panchatantra* easily accessible to the English speaking world. I have delved deeply into three authoritative, literal, translations of the complete text of the *Panchatantra* from the original Sanskrit by three eminent scholars: Arthur W. Rider (1925), Chandra Rajan (1993) and Patrick Olivelle (1997). Their work represents the best of what serious academics have to offer. I am clearly indebted to them. Nevertheless, the original in its entirety remains rather difficult to register and enjoy for non-academics. I have used their translations to understand and stay as close to the original of the *Panchatantra* as possible. Beyond that, the way I have organized the five books for a lay audience, the telling of the stories, the language used, and the summary of the wisdom highlighted by the stories, are entirely mine.

I have read and re-read the stories in various forms over the last fifty years. I wish I had a way of publicly thanking all the authors I have read on the subject of the *Panchatantra*. Suffice it to say, their work taught me that these ancient stories are the essence of Indian wisdom and values that deserve a wide international audience.

Throughout this venture, my husband Michael has been my strongest backer, my sharpest critic, my meticulous editor, and my most longsuffering love. I cannot thank him enough. I also owe thanks to my children, Kieran and Sean, who never failed to point out that my stories were not PC enough for children, and to my friends, Roland, Judy and Jon, who did not hesitate to point out that my story-telling was too confusing even for adults. I hope they will see that I took their judgments seriously.

I hope that my enthusiasm for these stories is catching. Cheers.

Narindar Uberoi Kelly, June 2014

MORE TALL TALES OF OLD INDIA

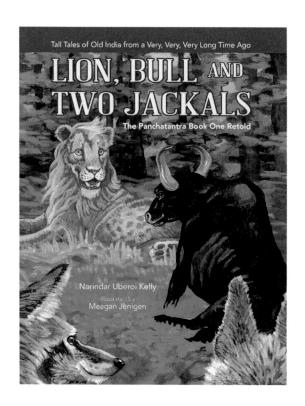

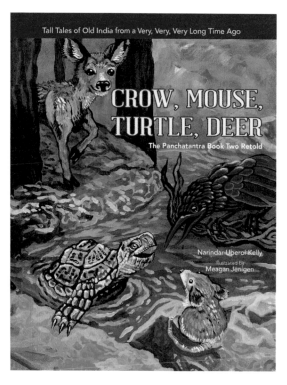

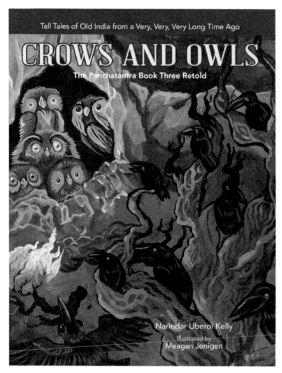

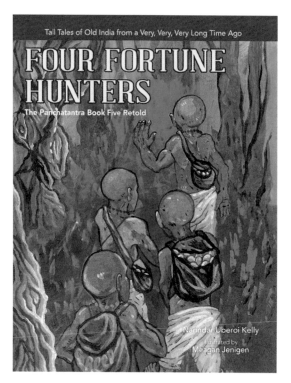

The Panchatantra Retold
Narindar Uberoi Kelly
Illustrated by Meagan Jenigen

CPSIA information can be obtained
at www.ICGtesting.com
Printed in the USA
BVXC01n2144200714
359735BV00001B/2